Wholeheartedly
For A Life Time

BY
Sunaina Verma

 pencil

ISBN 978-93-5438-417-2
© Sunaina Verma 2020
Published in India 2020 by Pencil

A brand of
One Point Six Technologies Pvt. Ltd.
123, Building J2, Shram Seva Premises,
Wadala Truck Terminal, Wadala (E)
Mumbai 400037, Maharashtra, INDIA
E connect@thepencilapp.com
W www.thepencilapp.com

DISCLAIMER: This is a work of fiction. Names, characters, places, events and incidents are the products of the author's imagination. The opinions expressed in this book do not seek to reflect the views of the Publisher.

AUTHOR BIOGRAPHY

A Dental Surgeon, a Fashion Model (Winner of numerous Beauty Pageants and represented my state in National level Beauty and Talent Pageant), a Martial Artist, an Artist (Got my first painting showcased in an exhibition at the age of 16), a Dancer, a Boxer, a sports person, a fitness enthusiast, a performer and most importantly a FOREVER LEARNER and now a Writer turned Author.

This is everything that I can think about myself at 5A.M. in the morning but I won't be wrong if I say that this is just 5% of who I am, there is still an ocean of fields unexplored and a personality unleashed... Working hard, learnering, falling apart and rising.

Contents

Night-Night

"Oh god! Where am I? Whose place is this?"

That's how I got up that morning, wearing nothing but a soft material shirt which was the only comforting thing that morning. I got up from the bed to find my clothes and leave that place ASAP..

You must be thinking its just a modern era bitch who got drunk last night and got up in someone else's house, someone else's bed in a complete wasted condition.

So fine it's just that but this hasn't happened to me before.

It's a shear silent scenario, feels like no one is here at this moment, I guess it's the accurate time to sneak out of this place. Uh! Supine position wasn't this informative, I can't even stand properly right now. I guess it's the whiskey taking revenge from me for mixing it with every single possible thing and gulping it like a dehydrated person gulping water in summers.

Fuck! This shirt and this bed is comforting...

I knew it wasn't my place and should probably get out of here without getting into any kind of troublesome situation but I guess my last night sins aren't allowing me to do so. Except for my head there wasn't anything that was making any sound so I decided to just get up and have a bath at an unknown place and in a strangers house but it appeared a neat place... nothing shaddy, everything settled and wow! The interior I must say that I got wasted for the first time and I didn't ended up in a dumpster is kinda achievement.

Okay. No time for kidding.. I betterget up, get a bath and leave. So I gathered all the energy that I could have had at that point and while walking towards the washroom I saw my dress (that I was wearing last night) nicely ironed, hanged on door and I think it wasn't just ironed but was probably washed as well coz it smelled fresh.

Wait... What? Is this a note? Wow!! a written note??

 "hey! Your phone died, I putted it on charging, And switched it on. You can find it on the Bedside table.

Your dress is all clean so you can leave ASAP

 just the way you want to. right now But most importantly You don't need to rush anywhere out of Embarrassment, no-ones gonna be at home And I would probably be gone till you get in Your senses but don't steal anything valuable. ;-) "

DON'T STEAL ANYTHING? Bloody. huh

This guy is weird, who leaves a note to a drunk lady in his house, who's place is this? Oh no!! My head. Uh! The bath and I'll leave then.

 So all fine, all settled about to leave I putted on my heals and then the mirror happened. No!! Last nights party dress, today at 11:00 in the morning? I'm just gonna take his shirt and anyway one shirt won't be a valuable thing anyway and Yeah!! His open cupboard is itself explaining that it isn't that valuable. So I took the white one. This guy really got an amazing collection of shirts I must say... Okay!! So one piece dress turned into a nice formal dress... If this guy got a nice sence of clothing then even Chris can pull any look out.

Okay. Hold on your horses Chris it's time to leave.

So I wrote THANK YOU on that same note overlapping his message. Well while leaving, I realized this guy had no pictures in his house and yeah no doubt he is a guy of quite a classy choice.

Oh! Another note? This guy is surely into getting girls to his place pretty often.

 "Heyya! All set to leave?

Don't forget to lock the door on the way out.

And put the keys under the 5th vase. he grey colored to be more specific."

"Okay you bossy shit." I exclaimed.

So I responded to this note as well in the same manner.

TAKING YOUR WHITE SHIRT ITS NOTHING VALUABLE I SUPPOSE

Oh! This guy? Seriously you had to choose the heaviest vase of them all? What are you? A MMA fighter? huh.

You know what Mr. I'm just gonna put it under any vase but not the 5th one. Get back home tired and know what struggle is.. after all it's the MBA last sem bitch you are trying to order.

Now what? Back to hostel? Or college?

Uhh it's 12, I better head to college...

The Corridor

"Krishna..." comes a shouting voice in the corridor, it was Rakshit, my fellow batch mate, a nerd and an amazing friend of mine from the very first semester, after all it's his kindness that he lend me his notes everytime and that is the only reason that I never had to attempt any exam twice. So he came running and stopped by my side and without catching a his breath.. he started blabbering questions in his single breath.

"Where you went from the party last night, you were so drunk, are you insane?? You left the party without me and without even informing me and why you didn't answerend any of my calls? Who do such things? When will you start acting mature, I was so worried about you and whe...."

"Hey enough... Cool down you question bank and it's Chris not Krishna, how many times do I have to tell you not to call me that in public?" I reacted in anguish.

"It's your name potato, you can't just change your identity everytime like last night.", Rakshit said trying to pull my leg or taunting me probably.

"And even you can't change the fact that it's *shit* in your name and in your head BOTH." I said trying to be all cool and chill like nothing major happened before and his questions are of no sense.

"It's you thats in my mind all the time so even you are cover in shit baby.", he said and laughed.

"Get lost", I said and pushed him away in a casual manner.

"Whateverrr.. C'mon tell me where you vanished last night? Everyone was looking for you, especially that Aniq guy." he giggled.

"Will you just stop it? I'm not in mood. Anyway why that idiot was looking for me? Wasn't he having his over possessive girl around?", I said rolling my eyes.

"Yeah she was there but I don't know he was like he wants to talk to you about some project or something related to last sem." he said in a casual way forgeting the fact that my all last semester projects were with him and not Aniq.

"Yeah sure." I said trying to end the Aniq topic.

"So tell me man! What happened?" Rakshit asked curiously.

"What happened?" I responded like I never left the party early and he was just too drunk to remember my presence in the party.

"You know what I mean. You were dancing when I saw you last and then I went to loo and the time I came back you were nowhere, I called you so many times and then your phone just got out of range."

"Frankly saying I don't know, I don't remember and I don't even want to know about it.", I told him with a hush-hush voice.

"You are making me feel worried, what happened?"

"First promise me you won't judge me."

"Look you are my only genuine friend here, you know I'm a dumb nerd, you helped me confess my feelings to my crush, we both stood for each other from the very first day of college, I love you, I'm worried for you man, please now tell me you aren't hurt.. I care for you, I'll never ever judge you... Yor hear that? Now tell me please.. Are you hurt? Did anything bad happened last night?"

"No. I'm all fine but I don't remember what happened last night and I woke up to this complete strange lavish, really lavish place and that person left me written notes.. can you believe that?"

"What?"

"What was it?"

"Someone's house, I guess."

"You guess?"

"Yeah I locked the door while leaving."

"You locked the door while leaving? You idiot you could have at least checked the name plate on the door. Tell me you checked it. "

"Yeah that I could have done but.. "

"but? "

"I was hungover"

"where this house was?"

"Okay don't kill me if I say I forgot that."

"You little piece of..."

"Hey!! Enough okay. I know I kind of messed it but it happens right?"

"Yeah it happens but do you remember you are engaged and would be marrying someone in the coming few months? And I don't think that things like that happen to girls like you."

"Do you remember that your mom think that you are dating some girl named Aish. Do you want me to tell her that, that Aish is the short of Ashish not Aishwarya or Ayesha?

"Why are you dragging my love life in between for no reason?", Rakshit said furiously and in a bit of afraid manner.

"Why are you making this a big deal for no reason? Let this be. I don't think anything happened anyway and even if something has happened then I will find it out and I promise that I won't be having my bachelorates in that case. Okay?"

"Okay. But I'm just concerned man, what if that guy turns out to be a psychopath killer who fell for you last night and now is probably stalking you?"

"Even better, he must be observing you around me all the time and would probably kill me out of jealousy or would kill you out of insecurity, what relief it would be."

"Stop!! Seriously stop."

"See whatever happened, happened, I don't even remember it so why to bother about it now, let's just go attend the class and act like nothing unsual happened. Can we do that? Please."

"Yeah!! You are right. Let's just get to the class and get our nice one hour nap sessions done like sincere K. G. students. (chuckles)"

The Grades

So things were finally cooling down, we were in the lecture hall tolerating some last interactive scenario with the faculties (it was more like sitting on the bench as if it's our living room, using our cellphones, calling each other names and what not on the name of interactive session because we were early and the marks were yet to be declared and yet to be discussed.)

" It's on the notice board, it's on the board, it's on the board. ", a guy from my batch came shouting in the class and ran back in the corridor.

People started running out of the hall, "I can't believe they made us wait for 3hours just for putting the grade sheet on the notice board." I uttered in mere disappointment.

"Yeah they could have just mailed us the marks, but what's your deal? We all know you are going to get an A+, like always." some batchmate muttered.

"Let's see.. I'm not a nerd after all." I claimed out loud in mere annoyance.

"Calm down, they are just jealous of you." Rakshit said.

"Yeah! Whatever. Now what you wanna do? I wanna go home and sleep." I told Rakshit.

"Don't you wanna see your marks? We all came to college for that only man." He asked.

"Its picture will be on the whatsapp group soon, and I just came for the interactive session.. Not this hurdle of reached to the notice board, pushing-pulling people around to see the marks." I said trying to make my point.

"Yeah!! My baby girl is right. So do you want me to drop you home?", He asked.

"Naah, you go spend time with Ashish, it's been long you guys haven't spent time together." I advised.

"I love you man, you take care of everything so well. I would have married you if you were a guy.. Trust me."

"Enough of this buttering man."

(Mobile notification sound from both the phones)

(Rakshit checks the phone)

"It's the mark list, isn't it?", I asked.

"Yeah!!" He said.

(Rakshit's mobile started ringing)

"It's Ashish, I better hurry, I'll see you, take care." he said and ran away.

(so I packed my bag and started walking out of the classroom when I realized that I should check my marks.)

"Fuck!!! How can this? Ughhh", I happened to react.

(I should head to Mr. Paghdar, he better tell me how and why I have gotten a B for my report?)

outside of Mr. Paghdar's office

I knocked his cabin door.

Knock-knock good afternoon sir, may I come in?, I asked in a polite manner even though my head was having a volcanic blast of its own.

"Yes, yes Miss Sharma, please", he approved.

"Sir actually I just saw the mark list.. And I'm quite not sure if my grade input is correct, if you don't mind can you please cross check it once?", I tried making my point without looking A++ hungry (I hope).

"No Krishna, it's fine I remember giving you a 'B-' and it must be that only but if you want I'll check it once."

He looked into some stuff under his desk cupboard and said "Oh! There must be some sort of printing mistake, it's a 'B', I'll get it corrected to B+ in ur mark sheet don't worry."

"Sir are you sure I'm not getting an A for my project, I have had worked really hard for it. Besides I always get that only, My presentations, my attendance and my reports are always on time and are always updated correctly" I said in a low voice... Craving for an A+.

"See Krishna, I have seen you do better, this project feels like you just did it, it's not how you have been doing your work. Don't get disheartened but I think your grades are marked accurately. Okay? And before you leave my cabin, umm I think you can keep this shirt, it suits you more." he said in kind of a decent yet flirty way if I'm not wrong.

"Excuse me?" I questioned.

"Yeah! I think you didn't read my notes but it's fine, this shirt looks just fine on you."

"It was your place? I was at your place last night?" I questioned in a sharp voice I guess because I was obviously shocked. Waking up to a strangers house was still fine but waking up in my professor's house, in his bed and showing up in college in his shirt. God what have I done?

"Yeah!" He said in a composed manner, adding "please lower your voice, I don't want people to gossip anything indecent about you or me."

"You owe me an explanation here Mr Paghdar."

"I do not owe you any explanation but you deserve to know what happened."
"I'll meet you in an hour, take your pick for the place and text me that to this number, I don't think we should be having such conversation over here, I hope you are getting what I'm trying to say.", saying that he handed me another note with his number written on it.

"We are meeting at your place in an hour SHARP and you text me the address. Okay?" I said in a low (coz I didn't wanted anyone to hear that either) yet confident voice (coz I wanted him to agree to this.. as if anyone would see us somewhere out together it'll be a hot gossip in itself).

"Okay miss." he agreed.

And I left his office.

Greet The Meet

I reached at his place and he was struggling with the vases just the way I wanted him to struggle but it wasn't funny anymore as this isn't just a guy but he is my faculty.. and to be honest.. I'm not as cool about it as I was acting in front of Rakshit and now I had to know everything so I went to him and pointed in the corner and said "pick up that red vase in the corner."

"Are you color blind to consider the red vase as the Grey vase? You could have got my place robbed.", he exclaimed in annoyed manner.

"And what are you a professor to leave notes for a drunk girl in your house?", I said in nervousness trying to make a sensible come back and realizing he is a professor and I'm making no sense.

He looked at me and passed me a straight face look and picked up the red vase. "Finally!! The keys." He said and didn't responded to my last sentence and I'm glad he didn't.

We went in, there was no-one, he asked "you need something to drink?"

No I'm fine, I responded. He said "make yourself comfortable I'll be back in a bit and there is kitchen if in case you change your mind and feel like having something." and pointed to the left and left.

It's been 30 minutes and he didn't showed up, I don't know if he forgot about me being here in his home? But it feels like that only.. I can't believe this, this guy lectures us about punctuality.? What nonsense...

I was bored so I went to his kitchen and got a soft drink cane from his fridge.

"So you changed your mind?", he chuckled.

"Yeah, as you changed your mind.", I taunted.

(He looked at me in a confused way)

"You were coming down in a bit, right? But you took like 45minutes." I responded.

"Yeah sorry, but I had to get fresh, this whole working day in that college in such humid weather is quiet annoying and also had to send some important emails.. I'm sorry for keeping you waiting.."

(He took out some vegetables and started chopping them while saying this and I never noticed before but he is really attractive and quiet young for being a professor in a college. Okay stop thinking this Chris and ask him about last night.)

"So Mr. Paghdar.. ummm.., do you mind telling me what happened last night?", I asked.

"Nothing.", he said casually.

"Nothing? Not even a thing?", I questioned.

"Nothing happened between us Chris and please call me Shantanu, I'm not your professor anymore, you completed your P.G. few days back. Remember?"

"Yeah!! I remember but how did I ended up at your place? And my clothes? Are you sure nothing happened between us?" I questioned him again.

"See I was coming out of the supermarket when I saw you drunk. I ignored you at first but then you started walking towards me and fainted, I looked around but I didn't saw anyone else there so I took you here just to keep you safe.", he said like its keep happening and it's not a big deal.

"What about my clothes? How they changed? I'm sure you don't have a fairy over here to do that."

"You puked the time I was taking you out of the car and then it was all over your clothes and mine too so I cleaned you up and that mess and my maid changed your clothes not me and I assure you I didn't did anything that I wasn't supposed to... You slept on my bed and I slept on that couch down here... Trust me on this."

"Thank you for keeping me safe when I wasn't conscious. I'm really grateful full about that.", I said this with all my heart.. being thankful to him.

"Don't mention it, I was raised in family of strong woman, they treated me well how a gentleman should be."

"Umm So you aren't married?", I asked.

"Where did that came from?", he chuckled.

"Just those notes that you left for me and now that you are cooking."

"Yeah.. well.. cooking is the basic need to survive alone and everyone should know.. but yeah!! I'm single and I live here alone... What about you?", he asked while he was still cooking.

"I'm... Umm.. Ah.. Can we please avoid this topic?", I asked.

"Don't feel shy to tell me about your relationship, I won't be taunting you in the viva about it.. C'mon but if you don't want to share then I respect that. It's your personal life and I'm no-one to question you about it.", he said.

"I'm.. Umm.. I'm.. Engaged and last night was more like my last celebration with my batchmates, give it to me I'll chop these.. you do the gravy.", I said while taking the knife from his hand.

"Aren't you very young to tie the knots?", he questioned.

"Aren't you my age to be my professor?", I cross questioned.

"Haha.. I'm sorry I shouldn't be judging. Well! I'm 26 and have done all my education and teaching is something I like so I'm doing it till I don't find any other job of my interest.", he answered.

So we talked while cooking and I don't know about him but I didn't noticed how the time passed so fast. The meal was cooked and he insisted me to dine in with him.. as I helped him prepare that I thought it's fine so I stayed and while leaving I took out his shirt from my bag (which I ironed and would have cleaned it too but had to rush to meet him so I just wanted it to look fine while returning it) in a paper bag and handed that to him saying "here, take it.", he questioned "what's this?".

I just said "open it" with a small smile.

"Oh no. Why?" he reacted. I wasn't able to understand this reaction of his as it was his shirt so I again questioned him "isn't it your favorite shirt? You said this in your office."

"Yes it is but it suited you more. Please keep it. Consider it as a farewell gift." he flattered me with these words, I can't believe but we had a moment there.

"I kept the shirt back in the bag and asked him "are we ever gonna meet again?"

"Obviously, we'll may be.. we are in the same field.. we'll cross our paths.. just don't stop working.", he responded and asked "how are you gonna get home now?"

"I'll take a cab.", I answered.

"Oh no no no no no, you are not taking any cab, it's late already, I can't let you go alone.", he showed his concern.

"No. Please. I have already troubled you a lot lately."

"Did I complained about that?", he questioned.

"No but..", he interrupted and said "Just give a minute I'm getting my jacket and then I'm gonna drive you home. Am I clear miss?", he questioned.

"Yes sir. Crystal clear." I replied with a smile that was cute according to me as he kinda looked flattered.

"Shantanu it is.", he said and ran upstairs saying "just a min."

He locked his home and we left, my house was about 7-10kms away from his place and it was 8.15 in the evening, traffic was bad so we eventually got another 30-45 minutes together. I was feeling a weirdly peaceful connection with him.

We reached.

He asked "aren't you gonna introduce me to your parents as the superhero who saved you from your own vomit?"

"Haha wicked humour, well I would have if I could have. I live here alone, my family is in Gwalior.", I answered.

He was just looking at me smiling like a baby. I don't know how it came out of my mouth but I asked him if he wanted to come up for a coffee may be. He was still smiling with those same expressions as if he wasn't capable of taking his eyes off me.

"Shantanu? Do you want to come over?", I asked again.

"Krishna, you are beautiful, good night, I'll see you soon." he responded exhaling a deep breath.

And that night ended there.

The Change

It's six in the morning, I don't have to go to college today and my concern now should be my future life and marriage as its the next month but I just can't stop thinking about Shantanu. He had his chance with me when I wasn't conscious, he and I spent the whole eve together, we were having such a nice time and we even had our own moment then why he didn't made a move?

I wasn't able to stop thinking about all this, I just couldn't.. even when I really wanted to. May be he isn't interested in me at all or maybe the fact that I'm engaged is bothering him but what about the night? He didn't knew about me being engaged then... May be he didn't did anything because I wasn't conscious and he anyway is a gentleman.

I really wanted to meet him again, spend my time with him like yesterday. There is something about him that I just can't put into words but what he made me feel is something that no-one has ever made me feel before.. not even Reyansh even though I'm getting married to him next month.

I was struggling, I wanted to meet him again but what if he doesn't feel the same?

I think I should text him but I won't be able to understand his actual reaction through texts but his voice can be judged.. Whether he is happy with my call or trying to avoid me would be clear then.

So I just picked my phone and right before pressing the green button on the screen I suddenly freezed, I didn't knew what would happen and I'm not sure whether this thought of mine is right or not but I really wanted to feel what I felt while looking into his eyes last night.

What the... Shit I can't believe I just dialed his number. Oh my god!! What am I gonna say?

(phone was still ringing... And then the sound comes "the person you are trying to reach is not answering the call please try after sometime")

Fuck. I don't believe it.. this guy is avoiding my calls.. what was even in my head?

(she throws the phone on the bed in mere irritation.)

I was panicking for no reason. If he has the balls to avoid me like nothing happened last night then even I don't care. Huh..

(she turned and walked to the dressing room and phone starts to ring.. She came back running to check who's call it is hoping it to be Shantanu's and when she picked up the phone and looked into the screen it showed *MR. PAGHDAR CALLING*.)

"Hello?", she just answered the call.

"Hey!! Hi!! You called? I'm so sorry I was in shower.", Shantanu said.

"Yeah!! Actually I was thinking.. ummm.. ", Krishna was unable to complete her sentence. And within seconds all of her anger was gone.

"hey!! You there?? Say something..", he insisted her.

"Yeah!! Actually I had a great time last night.. So I was thinking if you aren't busy or doing anything important than you can come and help me shop.. I'm actually not into this shopping stuff and everyone from college is busy packing their bags to go home. I'm drowning, please be the life guard Shantanu.", Krishna made up a reason out of nervousness of this unexpected call but she had to go shopping sometime.

"haha.. C'mon you could have just ordered me to accompany you Krishna.. I can't think of missing any opportunity to be with you..", he was blushing while saying that, his voice made it pretty obvious.

"so see you in 30min?", she asked.

"Sure. Pick you in thirty.", he answered.

Well this was easier than what I thought, Krishna thought while ending the call and started getting ready.

The Day After Yesterday

Oh my god!! Has he always been this smart or I just never noticed him before?, I questioned myself while looking at him from my window. He was doing something to his hair and then his shirts collar and then his sleeves and was again checking his beard in the reflection of his car window so I thought I should just go to him and embarrass him.. more like teasing him a lil.

"I can get you a hair dryer if you want to re-do your hair, or may be some compact or something. Actually anything. Tell me what you want? Don't feel shy.", I giggled saying this.

"Okay fine. Stop pulling my leg. In my defense I would just like to say- I'm not as pretty as you miss so I'm sorry if I'm looking stupid doing my hair in front of your house but I didn't wanted to make you wait so I rushed.", he said cute-ly.

"Okay. I grant you your life back and now you won't be sent to the life time sentence in prison my child.", haha I laughed while saying this.

"Thank you so much My Lord. I'm honored.", he played along.

We both started laughing and it was amazing, we barely spent ten minutes together but that happy vibe was already there.

Our eyes suddenly made a contact and I just felt like kissing him and I'm so sure he too had that feeling that moment. It was just so obvious through his looks.

"Shall we?", he asked politely after opening the car door for me.

I just nodded my head and sat in the car.

Shopping was just an excuse but it was more like we spending quality time together. Suggesting each other to try on some clothes and then waiting outside of the changing room to see each other in the clothes that we selected. We were in a mall.. things were going nice but then he noticed a horror movie poster and said 'hey let's go for it.'

"Are you made? Horror movie at this time? It's already six. I'm not into this.", I refused.

"aww chicken-chicken?", he tried messing.

In like five minutes we were making weird faces to tease each other while standing at the center of the mall, not realizing that this crowd may have someone that can recognize us and come up with some really shitty story of their own even though we were already having a movie like story of us making us thrilled.

We weren't really aware of the fact that someone has already spotted us in the crowd and that someone was Reyansh. If by chance I forgot to mention about him then let me just flash all the lights that I have on this fact that this guy named 'Reyansh' is my Fiance. Yes, I'm engaged to him only. And he even texted and called me that moment but I was so lost with Shantanu that all of those went unnoticed.

He didn't showed up then and didn't made things awkward like a nice person but what if he had to make things real dramatic like a daily soap afterwards.

Anyway... Unaware of this Shantanu and I were actually having a great time and he somehow convinced me to watch that horror movie with him.

Theatre was completely black and it was terrifying in itself and there were barely 5-6 more people otherwise all the remaining chairs were unoccupied.. we weren't able to see who those 5-6 people were as it was completely dark and we were equally horrified while watching the movie. I was hiding my face behind his shoulder and he was hiding his face behind the popcorn tub.

I must say that one should always get a popcorn tub for a horror movie, as the stuff in it is edible and when it's eaten then tub can be used to hide faces to avoid seeing any terrifying scene on screen.

Suddenly he just stopped moving when I hide behind his shoulder this time, I questioned out of fright 'Shantanu?', he didn't responded and stayed still. I asked again in a milder voice and pushed him a bit.. 'Shantanu? Are you alright?'. He still didn't responded. But his lips were moving as if he was trying to say something. I went a bit closer to him just to check on him. And the moment when I was close to him, he shouted 'blahhhhhhhhh' in order to freak me out. And I literally freaked and started to push him away saying 'I hate you, I was worried for you and all you thought of was to scare me?', I was still pushing him when he suddenly grabbed my hand from my wrist tightly and pulled me close.

Movie was still as scary as it had to be but we were having a romantic moment there. He touched my lips with his and said 'I'm glad you got drunk that night and I got to meet you this way.'

I kissed him back on his cheek and just held him closer and rested my head on his shoulder and we both started watching the movie again.

I just knew I was happy, and the moment movie got over we picked up all of our shopping bags and started to walk towards the lift when he asked me to just wait in front gate of the mall with half of the bags and he'll get the car from parking so I just nodded my head again and took my path thinking about the moment we just had and kept smiling like an idiot.

"Hey hon, how was your day?, came a sound from somewhere which I just avoided thinking, who's gonna talk to me that way here?

Then someone just called my name.. "Krishna?"

I turned around unaware that this could be Reyansh and not amused or happy but I was worried, I was afraid, I didn't knew what to respond or to say, I was freezed.

"Aren't you happy to See Me here?", he questioned with a strange face look.

"No. I'm just sh.. (was about to say shocked but managed not to utter anything stupid).

"Cmon. Why I won't be happy to see you? I'm just surprised to see you here like this.", and just hugged him to avoid any stressed convo here at least.

"Hmm.. For a moment I thought you aren't happy to see me here.", he said and hugged me stronger.

(My phone started to buzz in my pocket)

"Your phone..", he said.

"huh??"

"Your phone is ringing..", he told me.

(I took out my phone from the pocket, it was Shantanu's, he saw the screen)

"Who's Mr. Paghdar?", he asked.

"He is a friend of mine. He came to help me with the wedding shopping.", I lied and stepped aside telling him to excuse me for a minute.

I picked the call, "hey!! Come out, I'm here.", he said.

"Okay.", I said unaware of what I'm gonna tell Reyansh and Shantanu now.

"Hey all cool? You look tensed.", Reyansh asked.

"No. These bags are really heavy to handle in a single hand.", I made another excuse even though the bags were really not that heavy.

"Yeah. I'm so sorry. Give that to me.", he said and took my bags.

"Listen, actually Shantanu is waiting for me out to drop me home.", I told him.

"Let's go out and meet him then.", he said adding "is he a close friend?"

"I don't know about close but he is a good friend.", I told him.

Then we just walked out of the mall.

Shantanu was looking so happy when I saw him there waiting for me. He was still happy but his expressions quickly changed into a surprised look to see me walking out with someone else.

"Hey you just got a company.", Shantanu chuckled.

"Well not just a company but a forever company instead.", Reyansh said adding "haven't you told your friends about me yet? He questioned me and before I could even say anything and he introduced himself to Shantanu.. "I'm Reyansh, her fiance and you were just helping her to shop for our wedding which is next month and you are whole heartedly invited."

I was looking down at the floor, I wasn't able to see him even though I have had already told him about my engagement but what we shared these previous hours meant so much to me. It was all unexpected and unplanned. I had a feeling of him looking at me with so many questions to ask but I still couldn't look at him.

"Sure brother. I would love to come. You guys look amazing together.", Shantanu said smiling.. adding to it "Guys I think we should hurry, we are gonna get stuck in the traffic really bad if we don't leave now."

"Yeah, I'll just tell my driver to follow us and we should just leave together and have some quality time.", Reyansh said.

Shantanu agreed and I just nodded my head.

The Right Turn

"Excuse me? Who the fuck you think you are to sit at the co-drivers seat? From where you got this much of guts to seat with the person you just met. Krishna deserves to sit here it's her right. She is my girlfriend, Okay!! She is not my girlfriend yet but still she knows me more than u here and more importantly I know her and like her.", You should have kept your ass far-far-far away from this car and our lives. I changed the gear aggressively and I was shouting every single line that you read above but I was shouting that in my head cause technically he is her fiance and I don't know where I stand in her life right now. I mean we were having such amazing time together and what happened in the theater, that kiss. Oh man.. I'm in a mess.

I was so lost in my thoughts that I didn't heard what that piece of shit was talking about coz apparently he was talking to me.

"Sorry? You talking to me?", I questioned coz I didn't knew what else to say.

"Are you okay? I mean it feels like you are gonna get that gear in your hands in the coming few minutes. Does he always drives this way?", he asked to Krishna.

"No. He actually drives nice. It's just the hectic rush on the roads today.", she answered.

(Okay. So protecting me huh. It's Me-1 and that Wanna be-0)

"Ohkay....", Reyansh reacted in a hopeless voice as his joke or whatever he thought that is was.. wasn't entertained by either of us.

The silence in the car was so intense that I could hear them breath and then suddenly it started to rain heavily.

It was so romantic. I wish I had a magic wand so that I could just tap that on his shoulder and vanish him and spend this evening with Krishna.
Meanwhile I don't think there was any other sound in that car. We weren't talking, neither we were entertaining his blabbering much. I was about to take the turn to reach her house when he genuinely shouted "No. That's not the way to her flat."

"As far as I know this is the right turn." I said in a harsh voice and Krishna supported saying "he is right, that's the right turn." in kind of an embarrassed voice.

I think he sensed something. He was weird from the very second I met him but it was getting colder as if he felt the vibe that Krishna and I shared. I was about to drop her home and I didn't wanted to leave her alone with this guy. What if he does something to her or be rude to her or hurt her but why would he do that he is her fiance, he would get all romantic instead of doing that but what if he does both. I don't know what to do.. I never felt this helpless in my entire life till date. But why would he do something like that. He looked civil. But what if he questions her about me... What then? I hope I didn't got her in some kind major trouble even though I know what she must be feeling at this moment.

"Okay so umm thank you for everything Shantanu", she said in a mild voice.. Adding to which that creep said "yeah man thank you for accompanying her all this while and keeping her safe.. It means a lot.. Join us upstairs for some tea/coffee whatever you like.. What's say Krishna?"

"Yeah.. Please do..", Krishna said in hesitation.. It wasn't that obvious but I know she's feeling all awkward because of what happened between the two of us and then this sudden change I don't want her to feel the burden of reciprocation.. So I said "NO." in a cold manner just a no.

And I felt like it was rude.. I was being too rude cause obviously I was acting as her friend so I was definitely out of character so to cover that I instantly added.. "Its getting late.. I don't want to get stuck in the traffic again so I better leave now… But thank you I'll surely drop by sometime.." Tried adding a smile on my face.

"Okay!! then.." he said and stepped out of the car and opened the door for Krishna within seconds..

And I turned the car around and left. Really quick. I didn't wanted to but I couldn't stop thinking about her and Reyansh.. What if they get close and what if she'll like that.. I mean that's her fiance and he is probably staying there with her tonight and that's fine and even if something happen between them that's also fine they are adults and are officially engaged. Its fine.

But...

Whom am I kidding? Even if that's fine, I'm not fine with it.

HELLO-BELLO

"Brrrrrrrrrrrr... Brrrrrrrrrrrrrrrrr", my phone was buzzing, it was 11 in the morning.. I couldn't get up.. Reyansh stayed till midnight and left but I couldn't sleep last night so I didn't bothered answering my phone but I was up then thinking all about me and Shantanu..

But what was the sense of it, I was getting married with Reyansh within some days.. I should stop thinking about him but the way he touched me, it wasn't just a physical touch, he melted my heart every second he looked at me, smiled at me. That feeling was more like what a child would feel when you'll leave him in a room full of chocolates and video games. I can't explain it but I don't think I'll be wrong if I'll say that he touched my soul, everytime he looked into my eyes... Shantanu... Why you never met me this way before I got into this arranged thing? Why?

I can't let go of your smile from my mind when you realized you are kissing me.. That smile was so pure, pure happiness.. Free from lust, you were genuinely showing your love to me..

Well!! I'm in a shower and all I can think is of you, all I can see is your that smiling face, your sparkling eyes Shantanu.. I can't even keep the fact in my mind that I'm bloody engaged, I'm not supposed to get into all of this but now I'm and I have to get out of it.

From now on there won't be any Shantanu. No friend, no faculty, nothing...

I turned off the shower and overthinking right there and got out of my shower, unaware of how things are about to get..

And what could possibly distract you more than some hippy songs? So I picked up my phone and oh man!!!! 10+ missed calls??

It was Rakshits and few unknown numbers so I called back Rakshit and he immediately picked up the call and started blabbing "where were you I called you so many times, do you have any idea of what's going on here, Shantanu sir met an accident last night.. His condition is serious, where were you man?"

Within seconds I was in tears, I couldn't even say anything at that moment but I still gathered some courage and asked him about the hospital in which he was admitted.

I got in my clothes and rushed to that hospital clueless of what I'm gonna do there, what I'm gonna say to his family who am I? Why am I crying this much? To everyone I'm just one of his ex-student and no-one even know how much close we got in these few days..

I was outside the building of that hospital, thinking bout everything I decided today, that decision of being distant from him, that decision of not thinking about him, that very decision of not caring about him.. But here I am in tears, struggling to meet him and just to know if he is fine.. Because my presence there in this condition would be questionable and I don't know what I even mean to him. I don't know if he feels the same for me or not?

God!! Help me!!

"Chris?", I heard someone call my name..

"Hey!! Are you fine? We are here to see Shantanu sir..", Anisha (one of my batchmate asked)

They all were there to see him but they all looked fine, I couldn't even say a word when she asked if I was fine.. My head was processing so much at that moment that I didn't even realized that I know them, I have been around them from the last 5 years of my life.. Before I could have say anything, Rakshit jumped in and told them something and all of them went in the hospital.

He held my hand and I sobbed.. Something didn't felt right at that moment.. I couldn't help but I broke down in tears.. Rakshit was trying to calm me down but something didn't felt right..

His phone was continuously ringing.. He ignored those calls initially but then he made me sit in his car and checked his phone.. His face turned pale.

"Krishna look at me", Rakshit said adding to it "You are the strongest lady I know. Okay! You can't get weak, not now.. Not ever in your life.. I don't know what exactly happened between you and Shantanu Sir but now you have to let it go, your whole life is in front of you.. Please don't let these past few days make any change with that okay!?"

"I love him Rakshit, what I have felt with him isn't something casual.. Even if I want to deny this.. He and I have something.. It's peaceful when I'm with, its soulful when he looks into my eyes and its mere happiness when I see him getting all dull when we say goodbye after spending time together.. Even a good night was so painful for us just cause he had to leave me and go home and stay away till one of us gather the courage to ask the other one out.., I can't let go of what I feel for him.. Not now, not ever.. But I just can't go up and see him in pain, in that condition.. I love him.." I said sobbing and realizing that no ring and engagement can change what I feel for him..

"Krishna, let's go home.. You don't want to see him in this condition right now and I don't think he would like to see you this way either.", Rakshit tried convincing me to leave that hospital premises that time but I wanted to see him.

I gathered all my courage to face him, his family and accept him as a part of my life.. More than a professor, more than a friend.. I didn't knew about the consequences, all I knew was that I wanted all those feelings to feel throughout my life that I felt in those few days when we were together..

I got out of the car and walked in to the hospital, I was outside of his room and my batchmates were there.. They all were quiet, people were crying in there in the room.. I held the door knob to get in when Anisha told me that doctor informed them that he is in his last moments.. And I shouldn't interrupt a family situation but he could have been my family.. I went in there as quick as I could but stayed distant and when he saw me, he smiled, he called my name.. "Krishna is that you?" I couldn't control my tears and ran to him.. Held his hand and nodded my head.. "Hey!! I thought you would never come..", he whipped my tears and told me that "he loves my smiling face" in that moment he held my hand so strong that proved that what we had wasn't just one sided.. He had the same emotions for me..

Shantanu - "Krishna!! Grow.. Don't stop with your life ever.. My love is always gonna be with you in your heart.."

Krishna - "No.. I deserve a life with you, we just started.. please don't leave this quick.."

Shantanu- "I wish I could stay.."

Krishna-"I shouldn't have letted you go last night, it all my fault.."

Shantanu- "No, no, no.. Don't you ever dare to blame yourself for this... I love you from the very moment when you pucked in my arms.., Maa.. This is the girl I love, the only girl I have ever loved (he chuckled) and asked his maa, isn't she pretty..?"

Shantanu's Mom just nodded her head vertically, agreeing to him.. controlling her tears..

Shantanu just smiled and asked us not to cry if he die but always smile while thinking of him..

He closed his eyes, his ECG line turned into a straight line.

I walked out of the hospital.. I don't remember speaking to anyone that day at that moment… I walked to my home.. Blank.. And when I reached there I saw Reyansh sitting outside of my door..

Rayansh - "Are you fine? What happened? Where were you?"

He asked so many questions but I said nothing. I opened the door walked in, putted my bag and keys on the table I walked in the kitchen, poured a glass of water.. Drank it and walked towards Reyansh.

I sat on the sofa and asked him for the same.

Reyansh - "Speak up Krishna, what's happening?"

I took a deep breath and told him that Shantanu passed away.. He was shocked, he asked how? When? Where? I told him that it happened just an hour ago.. He met an accident last night... Before he could have said anything I pulled out my engagement ring from my hand and told him that I can't marry him, I apologized and asked him to leave.

Reyansh - "What?, just cause your friend died?"

Reyansh I don't hate you, you are a good person and I want to remember you that way only please don't say anything further. Shantanu was just my professor but I never knew I how I fell for him, that to in few days only.. And guess what? He loved me too..

I can't marry you, I love him and I always will..

That was the day when I saw Reyansh the last time, I don't know what he said to our families but no-one ever asked me any question neither taunted me about this failed engagement.

Its been 12 years now.. I see his family pictures on Facebook, I'm so happy that he is all settled in his life and doing fine with his career but I didn't married anyone.. I'm all settled, I earn well, I live on my own and I adopted a child, he is 15 now and someday I'll tell him about my love story.. *Where I once held the hand of my love and always kept its warmth in my heart.*